Pete the Cat

and the New Guy

GROOVY

Matthew 6:26–34
—J.D.

For my wonderful children, Trey & Destiny;
your talents and gifts inspire me! Mum
1 Peter 4:10
—K.D.

First published in hardback by HarperCollins Publishers, USA, in 2014
First published in paperback in Great Britain by HarperCollins Children's Books in 2014

1 3 5 7 9 10 8 6 4 2

ISBN: 978-0-00-759080-3

HarperCollins Children's Books is a division of HarperCollins Publishers Ltd.

Visit our website at www.harpercollins.co.uk
Printed and bound in China

Pete the Cat

and the New Guy

MOOHAUL MOOVERS

MOVING BOX

HANDLE WITH CARE

Kimberly and James Dean

HarperCollins *Children's Books*

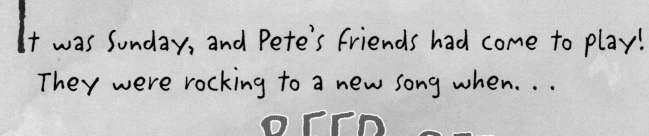

It was Sunday, and Pete's friends had come to play!
They were rocking to a new song when. . .

BEEP BEEP BEEP

There was a noise coming
from across the street!

Wise Old Owl had a view from his tree.
Pete said, "Hey, Owl! What do you see?"
Owl said, "All I see are green shoes and a red hat."
Pete answered, "Sounds like my kind of cat!"

Pete could not imagine who this new guy could be.
"I really hope it's a new friend for me."

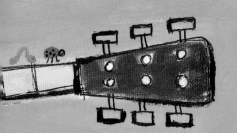

On Monday. . .
Pete wanted to say hi, but
he was feeling kind of shy,

so he just rode by and
by and by and by —

until finally Pete got to meet the new guy.

Pete said, "I've never met anyone quite like you!
You seem like a duck, and like a beaver too!"
The new guy said to Pete, "Hi, my name is Gus.
Glad to meet you. I'm a platypus."

Pete said, "You're not like me, and I am not like you, but I think being different is really very cool."

On Tuesday. . .
Pete and Gus took a walk down the street.
They came to Squirrel, who was playing in a tree.

"Hi, Gus," said Squirrel. "Climbing is easy. Try and see."

Gus gave the tree a try, but the branch
was way too high.
"I wish I could climb like you, but climbing
is something I just can't do."

Pete said,

"Don't be sad,
don't be blue.
There is something
everyone can do!"

On Wednesday. . .
Pete and Gus took a walk down the street.
They came to Pete's friend Grumpy Toad, who
said, "Come play leapfrog with me! Jumping is
easy. Try and see."

Gus jumped and leaped, but he couldn't get over Toad or Pete.

"I wish I could jump like you, but jumping is something I just can't do."

Pete said,

"Don't be sad, don't be blue. There is something everyone can do!"

On Thursday. . .
Pete and Gus took a walk down the street.
Soon they saw Octopus, who said, "Come juggle
with me! Juggling is easy! Try and see!"

"I wish I could juggle like you, but juggling is something I just can't do."

Pete said,
"Don't be sad,
don't be blue.
There is something
everyone can do!"

On Friday. . .
Pete and Gus took a walk down the street.
Gus said, "I can't juggle or jump or climb a tree.
It's no fun around here for me."

On Saturday. . .
Pete hoped Gus would come out to play.

"I wish Gus wasn't sad —
I wish Gus wasn't blue —
I wish there was something
we could do."

Just then Pete heard a groovy sound.
It was coming from across the street.
Gus was rocking to his own beat. SWEET!

Pete said,

"Check out Gus the Platypus.
He found something cool he
can do with us!"

TAP

"He's not sad,
He's not blue.

Gus found something that EVERYONE can do!"

Don't be sad! There's more Pete the Cat to read!

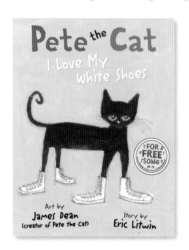
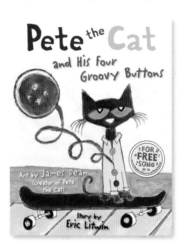